I Know Who You Really Are

Mary Minjares
Author

Beth DeHart
Illustrator

Morgan Michels
Production Editor

I Know Who You Really Are
First edition, published April 2022

Written by Mary Minjares
Illustrated by Beth DeHart
Production Editor Morgan Michels

Copyright © 2022

Hardcover ISBN 13: 978-1-95-268546-0

KITSAP
PUBLISHING

Published by Kitsap Publishing
Poulsbo, WA 98370
www.KitsapPublishing.com

Dedication Page

"This book is dedicated to all of my grandchildren. Thank you, Frankie, for sharing your story."

-Mary Minjares

"For my family who encouraged me, my friends who inspired me, and for my teachers who prepared me. I wouldn't be here without any of them."

-Beth DeHart

Dragons don't usually show up in the living room.
However, if a big brother tells his little brother that he
can't play too … a powerful dragon might show up.

Frankie loved playing with his big brother and it wasn't fair when his brother told him no. If a dragon stomped all over the room and threw toys everywhere, it wouldn't be Frankie's fault. Would it?

Dragons can really mess up a big brother's toys if they feel like it.

The dragon was very proud when he saw the mess he made ...

... until Gramma walked in.

Gramma gave him a gentle pat on his tail and said,
"I know who you really are," as she handed him some dragon snacks.

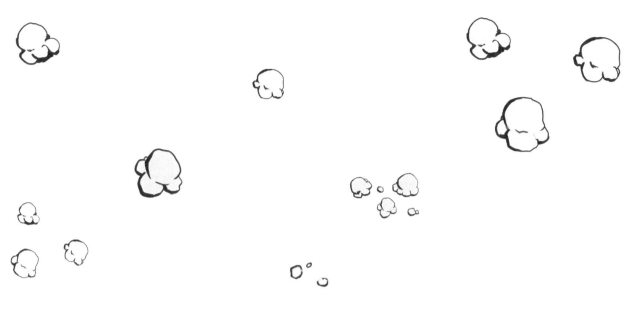

Frankie shared the snack with his
brother and together they picked
up all the scattered toys.

Fish don't usually float around the kitchen
inside of a wet, sloppy bubble.

But when someone has to take the recycling bin out and it's raining ... a fish might show up.

It was Frankie's turn for recycling but it wasn't fair!
If a fish splashed water all over the kitchen,
it wouldn't be Frankie's fault. Would it?

The fish was proud when he saw the mess he had made …

... until Gramma, wearing swim goggles,
stuck her head inside his bubble.

"I know who you really are," said Gramma, as she wiped up
the water and showed him the fish snacks she had.

Frankie and Gramma took the
recycling out to the garage together and
raced back to the house. Frankie won.

Bats don't usually show up under the blankets. However, if it's bedtime and video games aren't allowed for the rest of the night, a bat might make a cave under the blankets.

Frankie **LOVED** video games and it wasn't fair
that he wasn't ready to go to sleep.

If a bat showed up and wanted to play just one more game,
it wouldn't be Frankie's fault. Would it?

The bat was proud of how sneaky he was
but before he could even take his first turn,
Gramma crawled into the blanket cave.

She wore a flashlight strapped to her head.
"I know who you really are," she whispered,
as she pulled a book out from under her arm.

Together, Frankie and Gramma snuggled under the blankets. They took turns reading a bedtime story and shared a yummy bat snack.

Parrots don't usually go to school. However, if someone gets embarrassed and can't think of what to say, a parrot might show up.

Frankie raised his hand and it wasn't fair when he said,
"Red" when he **REALLY** meant to say blue!

If a parrot showed up and squawked, *"red, ReD, rEd, RED"* every time someone else tried to talk, it wouldn't be Frankie's fault. Would it?

The parrot was getting ready to fly far away when he heard someone singing, *"I know who you really are."*

Frankie saw Gramma in the schoolyard,
her arms stretched out like strong branches.

Frankie knew he didn't truly want to fly far away.

"*I like who you really are,*" Gramma said.
Frankie and Gramma walked home together,
practicing colors and sharing a snack.

CPSIA information can be obtained
at www.ICGtesting.com
Printed in the USA
LVHW071755060522
718108LV00011B/574

* 9 7 8 1 9 5 2 6 8 5 4 6 0 *